Originally published in French as *Les larmes* © 2019 Bayard éditions, France
Published in English in 2021 by Owlkids Books Inc.

Owlkids Books acknowledges the financial support of the Canada Council for the Arts, the Ontario Arts Council, the Government of Canada through the Canada Book Fund (CBF) and the Government of Ontario through the Ontario Creates Book Initiative for our publishing activities.

Published in Canada by
Owlkids Books Inc.
1 Eglinton Avenue East
Toronto, ON M4P 3A1

Published in the United States by
Owlkids Books Inc.
1700 Fourth Street
Berkeley, CA 94710

LIBRARY AND ARCHIVES CANADA CATALOGUING IN PUBLICATION

Title: Tears / Sibylle Delacroix.
Other titles: Larmes. English
Names: Delacroix, Sibylle, author.
Description: Translation of: Les larmes.
Identifiers: Canadiana 20200259202 | ISBN 9781771474221 (hardcover)
Subjects: LCSH: Crying—Juvenile literature. | LCSH: Emotions—Juvenile literature.
Classification: LCC BF575.C88 D4513 2021 | DDC j152.4—dc23

Library of Congress Control Number: 2020939449

Manufactured in Shenzhen, Guangdong, China, in September 2020, by WKT Co. Ltd.
Job #20CB0361

A   B   C   D   E   F

ONTARIO ARTS COUNCIL
CONSEIL DES ARTS DE L'ONTARIO
an Ontario government agency
un organisme du gouvernement de l'Ontario

Canada Council for the Arts
Conseil des Arts du Canada

Canada

OWL kids
Publisher of Chirp, Chickadee and OWL
www.owlkidsbooks.com

Owlkids Books is a division of bayard canada

Sibylle Delacroix

TEARS

Sometimes, when our hearts hurt,
our eyes fill up and we cry.

Everyone cries.
Little kids. Big kids.

Once in a while, grown-ups cry,

and crocodiles, with their
thick, scaly skin, cry too.

Sometimes even trees weep.

Crying cleans our messy feelings.

Some tears are quiet and slow,
slipping softly down our cheeks.

Some tears are so hot
they burst out in sobs,

and some tears are silent,
bubbling beneath the surface.

Sometimes we want our tears to be seen,

and other times we keep them to ourselves.

Our tears nurture secret gardens.

They are precious.

Small tears leave our cheeks salty.

Big tears leave our eyes puffy and red.

When tears threaten to wash everything away,

it's good to find arms we can cling to.

"It's okay now."

After we shed one tear, two tears,
every tear we hold inside . . .

we feel lighter,
ready for new adventures.